CORN DISCLAIMER

This is Kevin's first book dealing with what chickens eat. Kevin knows that chickens eat cracked corn. "Cracked corn" is dried corn kernels that have been removed from the cob. Kevin knew what "cracked corn" was, but he couldn't figure out how to draw great piles of dried kernels. He thought that it would look better if he drew the corn still on the cob. He's sorry if this bothers you. He also promises never to do a book about chicken feed ever again.

For Kim "the Title Maker" Norman

First published in the United States of America in 2007 by Walker Publishing Company, Inc.
Distributed to the trade by Holtzbrinck Publishers

For information about permission to reproduce selections from this book, write to Permissions, Walker & Company, 175 Fifth Avenue, New York, New York 10010

Library of Congress Cataloging-in-Publication Data available upon request
LCCN: 2007003706
ISBN-13: 978-0-8027-9684-4 • ISBN-10: 0-8027-9684-2 (hardcover)
ISBN-13: 978-0-8027-9685-1 • ISBN-10: 0-8027-9685-0 (reinforced)

Typeset in Elroy
The art for this book was created using 140 lb Arches watercolor paper, Higgins waterproof black ink, and assorted pen nibs. The art was scanned and PhotoShop was used to place color.

Visit Walker & Company's Web site at www.walkeryoungreaders.com

Printed in China
10 9 8 7 6 5 4 (hardcover)
10 9 8 7 6 5 4 3 2 (reinforced)

All papers used by Walker & Company are natural, recyclable products made from wood grown in well-managed forests. The manufacturing processes conform to the environmental regulations of the country of origin.

GIMME CRACKED
CORN &
I WILL SHARE

Kevin O'Malley

Walker & Company ◆ New York

One night Chicken had a dream.
He dreamed that in a beautiful barn,
buried under a great pink pig,
was a treasure of cracked corn—
all the corn that any chicken could ever want.

YUM!

Chicken couldn't stop thinking about the cracked corn.

So the next morning Chicken set out to follow his dream.

"Where are you going?" asked George.

"I'm going to find that beautiful barn. Do you want to go with me?" asked Chicken.

Well, I have been feeling a little cooped up lately.

Chicken and George walked along a hot and dusty path.

"I don't think this is a good day to be traveling," said George.

"What do you mean?" asked Chicken.

It's Fry-day!

Chicken and George
came to a road.
How did the chickens
cross the road? you ask.
They crossed at
the light.

They walked across a playground. "Is this why we crossed the road?" said George.
To get to the other slide?

As they walked past a basketball court, they heard the referee call a foul. But he wasn't talking to them.

Chicken and George crossed a great open field.
Suddenly a cat appeared.
"Here he comes!" shouted Chicken.
"Make like an egg on a hill," shouted George.
"What do you mean?" shouted Chicken.

They hid in a scary forest.
But a hawk attacked them.
"What do you call a chicken that can swim?" asked George.
"I have no idea," said Chicken.

DUCK!

They raced out of the forest and into town.

"Maybe we should stop in here to hide," said Chicken.

"I think we should keep running," said George.

"Why?" asked Chicken.

Chicken and George were tired. They traveled all day and through the night.

Finally when the sunny side came up, they found the beautiful barn—home of the great pink pig.

"Okay," said Chicken, "you kick the pig and get him to chase after you, and I'll start digging for the treasure."

"You've got to be kidding," said George.

"What are you—chicken?" asked Chicken.

As a matter of fact, yes.

The argument woke the giant pig. He looked at the chickens and asked, "What do you two want?"

Chicken told him about his dream.

"Why do you want the corn?" asked the pig.

"Because it's what chickens grow on," said George.

I thought they grew on egg-plants.

"Would you mind getting up?" asked Chicken.

"Listen," said the pig. "I had a dream once. And in my dream I sprouted wings. I flew to a far-off place where there was a chicken coop, and buried under the chicken coop there was a treasure of sweet cracked corn. But I didn't go look for it because it was JUST A DREAM. Now go away!"

Chicken thought about what the pig had said as they walked out of the barn.

"I guess this trip was a waste," said George.

"Why?" asked Chicken.

The minute they got back home, Chicken started to dig under the chicken coop.

All the animals on the farm gathered to watch.

A horse said to George, "I had an uncle who thought he was a chicken. My aunt would have divorced him . . .

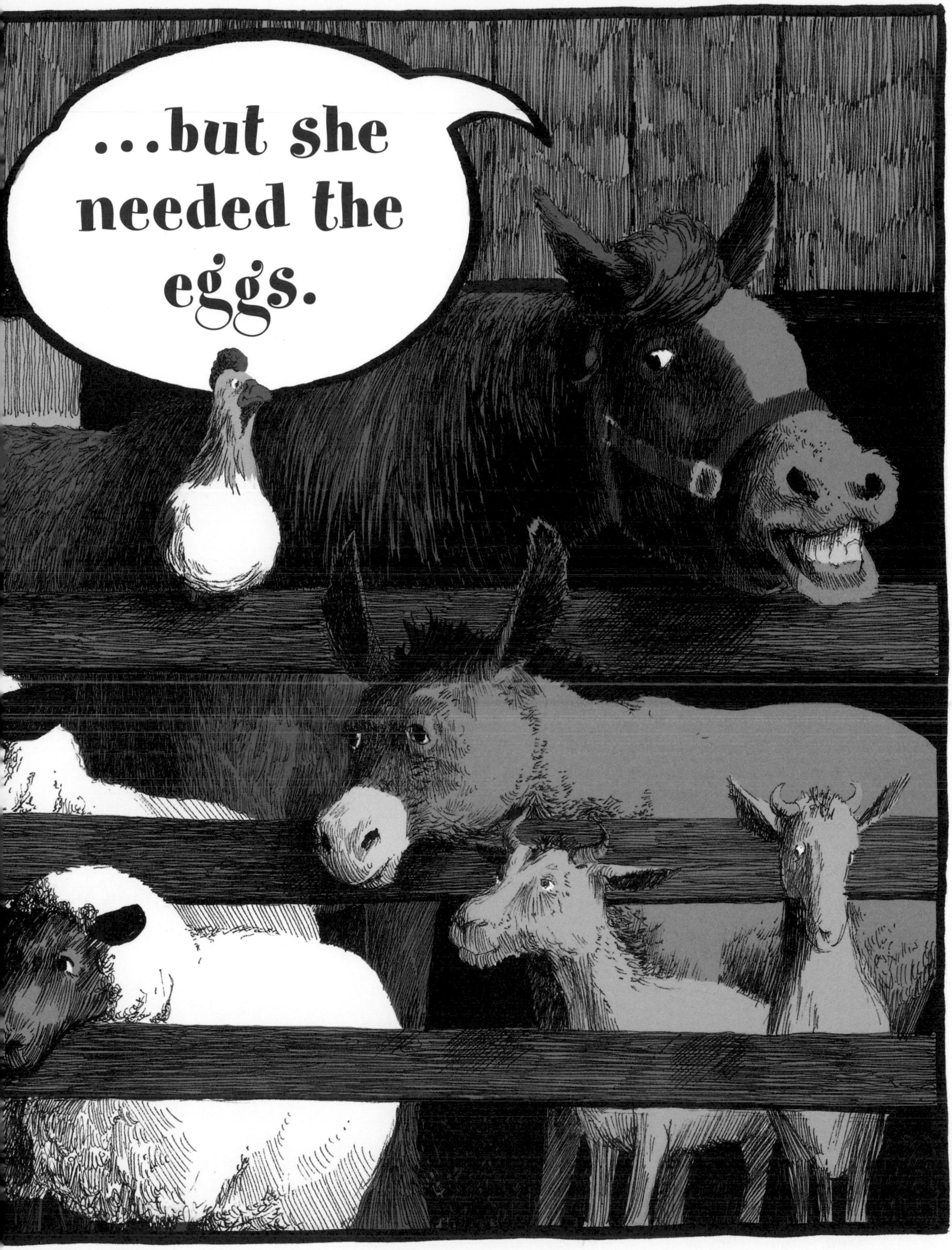
...but she needed the eggs.

After a few hours of hunting and pecking, Chicken found the treasure.

Ear after ear of cracked corn came flying out from under the chicken coop.

Egg-stra-ordinary!

When Chicken was done digging up the treasure, all the farm animals gathered around and had an egg-ceedingly egg-squisite egg-sample of an egg-stremely egg-ceptional feast.

E
OMA

O'Malley, Kevin.

Gimme cracked corn &
I will share